Brother Wolf,
Sister Sparrow

Brother Wolf, Sister Sparrow

Stories about Saints and Animals

RETOLD BY

Eric A. Kimmel

ILLUSTRATED BY

John Winch

Holiday House / NEW YORK

For Noelle

E. A. K.

For Dr. Maurice Saxby,
a master of story

J. W.

Text copyright © 2003 by Eric A. Kimmel
Illustrations copyright © 2003 by John Winch
All Rights Reserved
Printed in the United States of America
www.holidayhouse.com
Text type is Palatino.
The art was created with acrylic paint
on handmade French paper.
The chapter opening borders were created
by Jessie Winch in Photoshop.
The author's principal source for this book is *Butler's Lives of the Saints*
(New York: P. J. Kennedy & Sons, 1956).
First Edition

Library of Congress Cataloging-in-Publication Data
Kimmel, Eric A.
Brother Wolf, Sister Sparrow: stories about saints and animals /
collected and retold by Eric A. Kimmel; illustrated by John Winch.—1st ed.
p. cm.
Contents: Saint Ambrose and the bees—
Saint Blaise and the animals—
Saint Brendan and the whale—Saint Brigid and the cows—
Saint Francis and the wolf—
Saint Giles and the doe—
Saint Hormisdas and the camels—
Saint Hubert and the stag—Saint Hugh and the swan—
Saint Kevin and the otters—
Saint Martin and the goose—
Saint Notburga and the pigs.
ISBN 0-8234-1724-7
1. Christian patron saints—Legends. 2. Animals—Folklore.
[1. Saints—Legends. 2. Animals—Folklore.]
I. Winch, John, 1944– ill. II. Title.

PZ8.1.K567 2003
398.22—dc21   2002027303

CONTENTS

Irish
3 Brendan
4 Bridget

10 Kevin

Sermon to the Birds
Saint Francis of Assisi

Birds, my sisters, you are very precious to God, Who created you, and you must always praise Him, all the time, everywhere you go. He gave you feathered clothing. He gave you freedom to fly wherever you will. He also kept you safe in Noah's Ark, to preserve your species.

You, in turn, have a special link to Him, for you fly in the sky. Other than this, you neither sow nor reap. But God loves you all the same and gave you rivers and springs to quench your thirst. He gave you mountains and valleys for shelter, and tall trees for building your nests. You have no need to weave or sew, for God dresses you and your children.

God loves you in a special way. That is why, dear sisters, you must never be ungrateful. Always try to praise God's name.

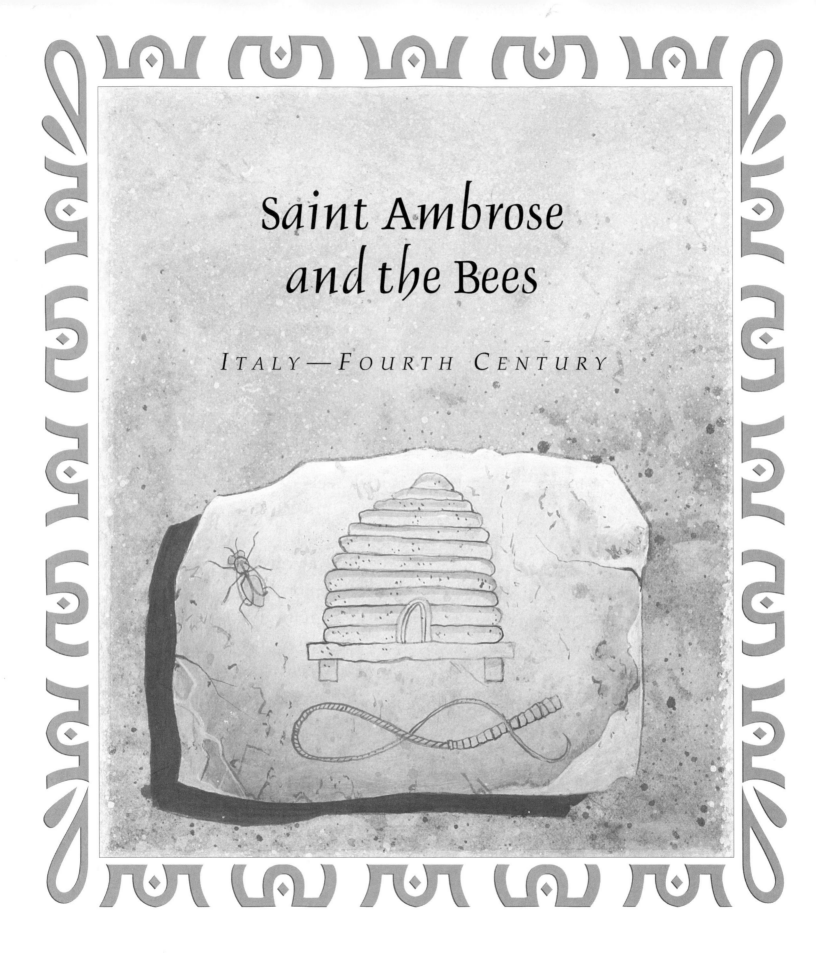

Saint Ambrose
and the Bees

ITALY—FOURTH CENTURY

When Saint Ambrose was a baby, something strange occurred. As he lay in his cradle one warm summer day, a swarm of bees flew in the window and clustered around his mouth. The bees didn't sting the baby or hurt him. Baby Ambrose was not frightened at all. Instead, he laughed as the swarming insects tickled his face.

The frightened nurse ran to fetch Ambrose's parents. His father decided to wait for the bees to leave. Sure enough, within minutes the bees flew away through the same window by which they had entered.

In those days people believed that unusual events were signs of things to come. What did this strange swarm of bees clustered around a baby's mouth mean?

Ambrose's parents consulted a famous oracle, who told them they had nothing to fear. They should rejoice, for God had given their son a great gift. The bees swarming around his tiny mouth meant that he would grow up to become a famous writer and speaker, one whose words would be as sweet as honey.

The oracle's prophecy came true. Ambrose grew up to become one of the most famous speakers of his time. The Roman emperor appointed him governor of a province. He ruled from Milan, its capital city.

One day the bishop of Milan died. The leaders of the church met to choose a new bishop. There were two candidates for the position. Neither held a clear majority. Their angry followers jostled one another, threatening violence if their favorite candidate was not elected.

Ambrose entered the church. The angry crowd fell silent as the governor addressed them in a clear, ringing voice. He urged them to settle the matter in the spirit of peace and friendship.

Suddenly someone in the crowd shouted, "Why not make Ambrose our bishop?" The others took up the cry. "Yes! We want Ambrose! Ambrose, bishop! Ambrose, bishop!"

Ambrose never expected this. He was a governor, not a churchman. Although he had worshiped as a Christian all his life, he had never been baptized. How could one who was not formally a Christian become a bishop?

In the end Ambrose's family and friends persuaded him to accept the will of the people and the will of God. Ambrose had himself baptized and accepted the role of bishop. He went on to become one of the Church's greatest leaders and teachers.

Saint Ambrose's feast day is celebrated on December 7. His emblems are the beehive and the whip, for he taught that sweetness must always be tempered with firmness. He is the patron saint of learning.

Saint Blaise
and the Animals

ARMENIA—FOURTH CENTURY

Saint Blaise was a remarkable child. His wisdom and goodness so impressed his elders that, while he was still a young man, they elected him bishop of the town of Sebastea. The Christian community there grew as people flocked to listen to Blaise preach.

Blaise's growing reputation attracted the attention of the pagan Roman governor, Agricolaus, who hated Christians. He decided to root out the growing Christian community by doing away with its leader. He sent soldiers to arrest Blaise.

Before the soldiers arrived, Blaise received a warning from heaven. An angel appeared, telling him to flee to the mountains. The angels guided Blaise to a remote cave. Here he found shelter and safety among the wild animals of the forest.

Blaise preached to the wild animals, healed their wounds, and gave them medicine when they were sick. Rabbits and foxes lay down together; bears and fawns nestled side by side to listen to Blaise preaching. Birds perched on his shoulders. Poisonous snakes curled around his wrists and ankles as he spoke of God's love for all creatures.

One day hunters arrived at the cave. They had been sent by the governor to catch animals for the Roman games, in which animals and human beings fought to the death. Blaise pleaded with the hunters to spare his animal friends and offered himself in their place. The hunters took Blaise away, knowing that the governor would pay them a rich reward for capturing the fugitive bishop.

Even as he marched toward a cruel death, Blaise continued to work miracles. A poor woman came up to him, complaining that a fierce wolf had stolen her pig. Blaise went to the edge of the forest. He called out to the wolf to return the woman's pig. Within minutes the wolf appeared, carrying the pig in its jaws. It laid the unhurt pig at the woman's feet, licked Blaise's face and hands, then trotted back into the forest.

Another woman approached him, carrying her son, who had choked on a fish bone. Blaise prayed over the boy, and after the bone miraculously popped out of his throat, the boy came back to life.

The governor ordered Blaise whipped, then thrown into a dungeon without food, water, or light. Yet the people whom Blaise had helped found ways to smuggle in food, wine, and candles.

The governor then ordered the bishop tortured to death. Soldiers raked Blaise's skin with sharp iron combs used to straighten fleece. Although bleeding from a hundred wounds, Blaise prayed to God to forgive the governor. The outraged Roman ordered that Blaise's head be cut from his body.

Saint Blaise's feast day is celebrated on February 3. Because of the manner of his death, he is considered to be the patron saint of weavers and wool carders. He is also the patron saint of wild animals because of his kindness to them. His emblem is the fish because he saved the life of the boy who choked on a fish bone. It is also the reason why people gather in Catholic churches on Saint Blaise's feast day for the Blessing of the Throat. Saint Blaise is regarded as the special protector of throats and people who have throat trouble.

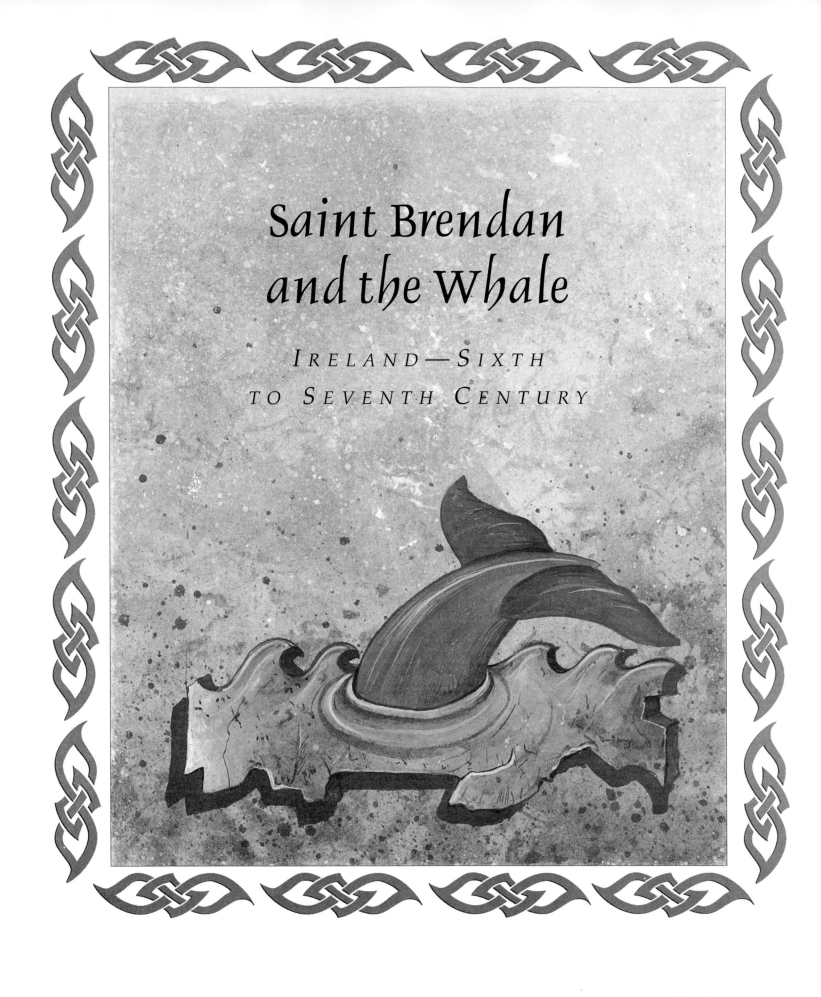

Saint Brendan
and the Whale

IRELAND—SIXTH
TO SEVENTH CENTURY

Saint Brendan was one of the most widely traveled men of his age. He left Ireland and visited Scotland, Wales, and Brittany, establishing monasteries and holy communities wherever he went.

Then Brendan felt the call to travel farther, beyond the vast unknown ocean west of Ireland. He wanted to bring God's word to the people who lived beyond the horizon.

Brendan and sixty of his monks set sail in basketlike boats called curraghs. Once, according to legend, they came upon a mysterious island in the middle of the sea. They stopped to go ashore to celebrate Mass. There was no sand, and barnacles covered the ground beneath their sandals. A warm mist enveloped them. It appeared to come from a hole at the head of the island. "What strange place is this?" the monks asked Saint Brendan.

Before he could answer, the island began to move. For it was no island at all but an enormous whale. The monks ran to their boats. No sooner had they all gotten in than the whale dived to the bottom of the sea. Brendan led his companions in a special Mass, thanking God for delivering them from peril.

Later, it is said, the whale carried Brendan and his companions across the sea to an unknown land. People with coppery-colored skin and straight black hair came down to the beach to welcome them. Brendan preached to the people about God. Although they could not understand his language, he believed that his words reached them. Brendan and his monks erected a large cross on the beach. Then they got back on the whale and returned to Ireland.

Did Brendan and his Irish monks discover America nine hundred years before Columbus? There may be some truth to the story. When the first Vikings came to Iceland, they encountered a community of Irish monks already there. Perhaps the monks had gone farther west? In 1976 the explorer and author Tim Severin sailed from Ireland to America in a curragh very much like Saint Brendan's to prove that it could be done.

Saint Brendan is the patron saint of sailors. His feast day is May 16, and his emblem is the whale.

Saint Brigid and the Cows

IRELAND—FIFTH TO
SIXTH CENTURY

Saint Brigid's father was a wealthy man who owned a large herd of milk cows. When Brigid was a little girl, her father sent her to milk the cows and churn the milk into butter. Brigid herded the cows together, then milked them one by one. She poured the rich, sweet milk into a churn and began turning.

As the handle of the churn moved up and down, Brigid sang in time to its rhythm. People passing by on the road stopped to listen. Many were poor, dressed in rags. Listening to Brigid's song helped them forget their troubles.

Brigid churned the milk into butter in no time at all. She scraped the sweet butter, yellow as a field of buttercups, out of the churn. She had enough to fill a bucket. Then she noticed the poor people standing in the road. They thanked her for the music.

Brigid could not feel happy, seeing how ragged and starved they looked. "Would you like some butter?" she asked them.

The poor people looked at her with grateful eyes. Brigid held out her bucket to them. The butter tasted so good! More people came. Soon the bucket was empty.

"I'll make more," Brigid said. "And would you all like a drink of fresh milk too?" She milked more cows and churned more butter, singing all the while. She spent the whole morning and a good part of the afternoon milking and churning. She poured gallons of milk and churned pounds of butter. And the miracle was that her cows kept giving milk until all the poor people had enough.

By then both churn and butter pail were scraped clean, and not a single drop of milk was to be had from any of the cows.

"It's time to go home. Father will be wondering where I am," said Brigid. She picked up her churn, pail, and milking stool and started back down the road.

Her father was indeed wondering and not just about Brigid. "Where is the butter?" he asked as she came through the doorway.

"Gone," said Brigid.

"Gone? How can it be gone? What about the milk?"

"It's gone too!"

"All those cows? All that milk? All that butter? Gone, you say? Where did it go?"

Brigid told her father how she had spent the day pouring milk and churning butter for the poor people who had come by on the road. Now there wasn't a drop of milk or a pat of butter to be had. But indeed, wasn't it worth a little milk and butter to make all those poor souls happy?

"No! It wasn't worth it at all. And you're a fool," her father said. "If you give to every beggar who comes wandering down the road, we'll soon have nothing for ourselves. What will become of us then? Let this be a lesson to you. Go back to the pasture, and don't come home until you've replaced all the milk and butter you've given away."

Brigid picked up her churn, bucket, and milking stool and returned to the pasture. She found the cows bedded down for the night. There would be no more milk until tomorrow. Brigid sat down on the stool and looked up toward the sky.

"Heavenly Father," she said, "I always try to do good, but I am not sure if I've done right or wrong. I tried to help the poor. Now

Father is angry with me for giving away our milk and butter. Was I wrong? Or is he? Please show me the right way. Give me a sign."

As soon as Brigid finished her prayer, she heard wings rustling overhead. Coming down from heaven was a flight of angels. Each one carried a bucket, a churn, and a milking stool. The angels set their stools beside the cows, sat down, and began milking. When their buckets were full, they churned the milk into butter—three times as much butter as Brigid had given away. Then they flew back to heaven, leaving the butter behind in buckets of purest gold.

Thus did Brigid receive her sign. And thus too did she learn that no good deed is ever wasted. It always returns to the giver tenfold.

Saint Brigid is one of Ireland's most important saints. She is the patron saint of milkmaids. Her feast day is February 1, and her emblem is the cow.

Saint Francis and the Wolf

ITALY—TWELTH TO
THIRTEENTH CENTURY

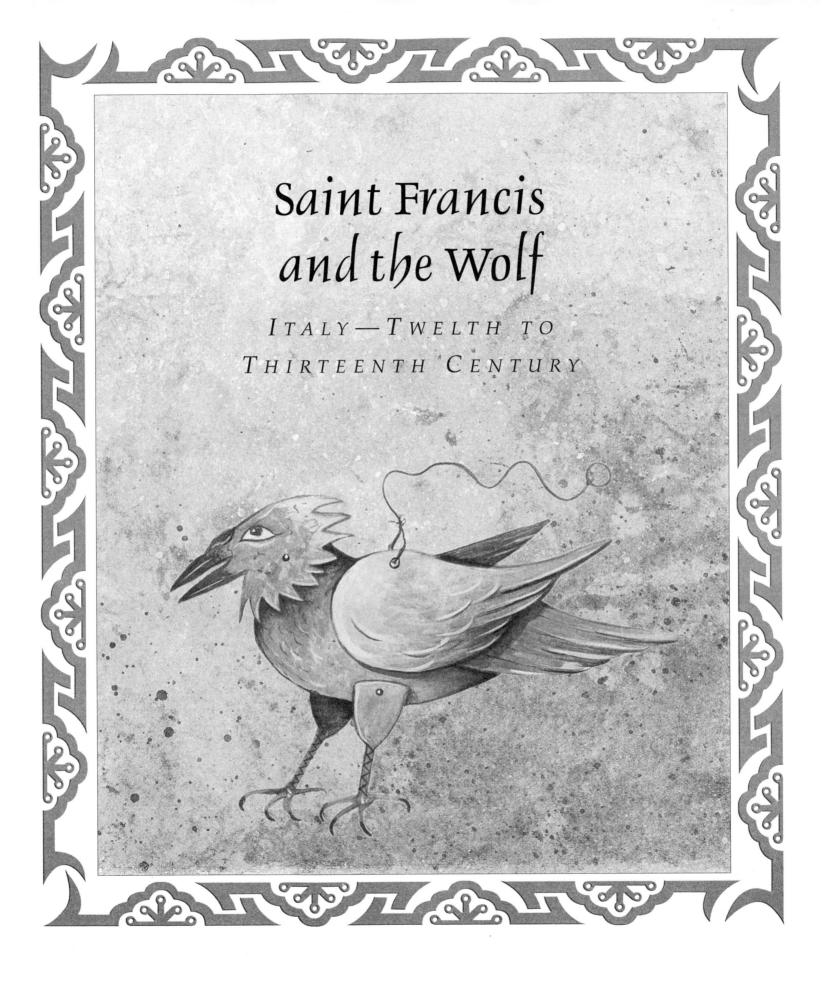

Francis of Assisi is one of the most beloved of all the saints. The son of a wealthy merchant, he abandoned a life of luxury, giving away all his possessions to devote his life to God.

Love for all creation filled Francis's heart. He preached not only to people, but to birds and animals, addressing them all as "brother" and "sister."

Francis once traveled to the town of Gubbio. The farmers he met along the way warned him about the neighboring forests, which were filled with savage wolves.

Francis did not let the warnings frighten him. He said, "I have never done these creatures any harm. Why would they harm me?" The farmers thought Francis must be crazy. They did not understand his belief that love is stronger than fear.

Francis arrived in Gubbio. The streets were deserted. No one dared leave the house, even in the middle of the day. The people of Gubbio lived in constant fear of a ferocious wolf that lurked in the surrounding hills. The wolf had killed the hunters sent to capture him. He was so bold that he came into town, snatching anyone he found in the streets. He carried his screaming victims off to his den. None of these poor people were ever seen again.

The people of Gubbio begged Francis to rid their town of the menacing wolf. Francis agreed to try. However, he told the people that he would not harm or kill the animal. If he could convince the wolf to agree to live in peace with the townspeople, would they in turn agree to live in peace with the wolf? The people of Gubbio offered to do whatever Francis asked.

Francis walked out of town, alone. As he entered the forest, he suddenly heard a fierce growl. The biggest wolf he had ever seen stood before him in the middle of the road. His yellow eyes gleamed. Foam dripped from his fangs as he gathered himself to pounce.

Francis did not try to run away. He turned to the wolf and smiled. Raising the wooden cross that he always carried, he spoke gently to the animal.

"Brother Wolf, I know you have done some terrible deeds, but I also know that you had no choice. You were hungry and wanted to eat. I feel so sorry for you. It must be terrible being hated and hunted all the time, to have to kill other creatures because others want to kill you. May I show you a better way? If I can convince the people of Gubbio to live in peace with you and provide meat for you to eat, will you agree to live in peace with them? Show me, Brother Wolf, that you understand my words. Show me that you will honor this promise."

The wolf cocked his head. Then he rose on his hind legs, placing his paw in Francis's hand.

Francis hurried back to Gubbio. He told the townspeople of his encounter with the wolf and the bargain he had made with him. From that day on, the people of Gubbio set out platters of meat by the fountain in the town square. The wolf came into town every day to have his meal. He ate only the food provided for him. He never harmed or threatened another living creature again.

Saint Francis of Assisi is the patron saint of animals and those who work to protect them. He is also the patron saint of Italy. His feast day is October 4. Birds are his emblem.

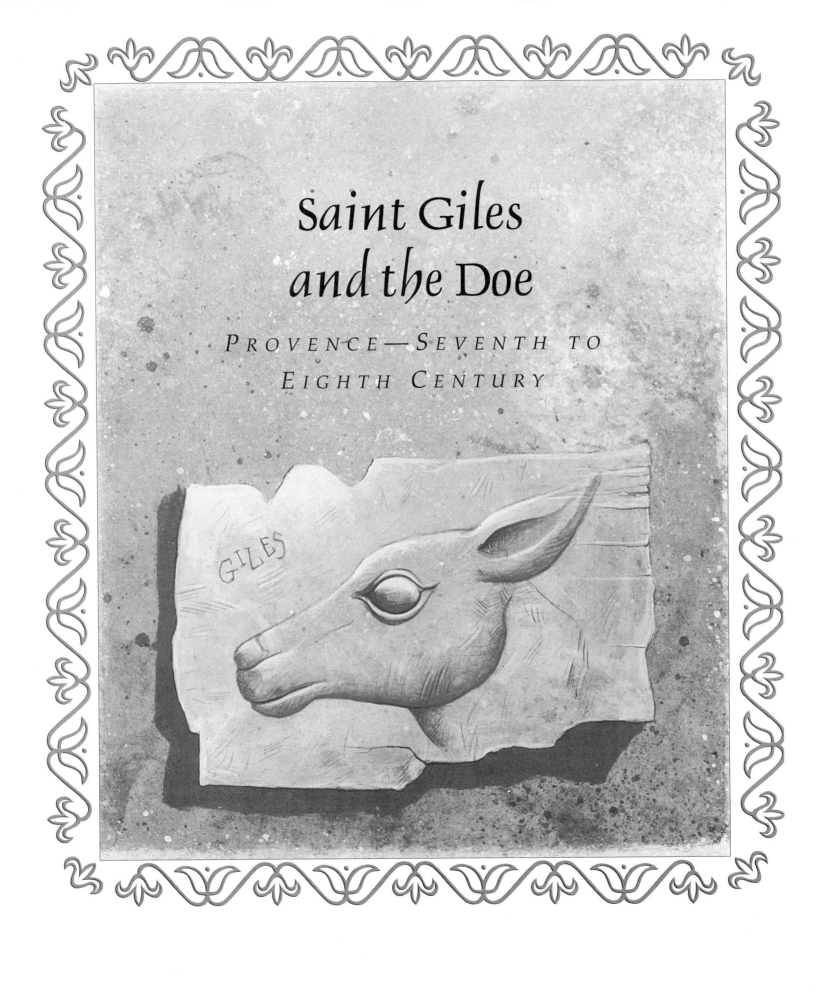

Saint Giles
and the Doe

PROVENCE—SEVENTH TO
EIGHTH CENTURY

Saint Giles was a hermit who lived in a hut deep in the forest. Here, far from human beings, he devoted himself to a life of holiness and contemplation.

Giles became a great friend to the animals that inhabited the forest. Deer and foxes, wolves and bears came to his door. Giles groomed their fur, healed their wounds, nursed them when they were sick. The animals loved Giles. They brought him food to eat and protected him from danger.

One day Emperor Charlemagne came to the forest to hunt. His hounds startled a white doe. The emperor and his party galloped off in pursuit.

The frightened doe ran to Giles's hut. "Do not fear, gentle friend. No one will harm you," the hermit said as the emperor's hunting party came into view. "Do not harm this gentle creature. She has begged me to protect her, and I will," Giles told the huntsmen.

Charlemagne fitted an arrow into his bowstring. "Step aside, hermit! That doe is our rightful prey. I have made a vow to kill her. And I will!"

"Then you will have to kill me as well, for I will not step aside." Giles raised his face to heaven, his eyes closed in prayer.

Charlemagne shot his arrow, thinking the hermit would surely jump aside. Giles never moved from his spot. The emperor and his party looked on in horror as the arrow struck the holy hermit's breast. Giles fell to the ground, bleeding from a terrible wound.

Charlemagne leaped from his horse. He cradled the hermit in his arms. "Forgive me, holy man," he begged. "I did not mean to harm

you. Now I am guilty of a great sin. Heaven will surely punish me."

"I forgive you," Giles murmured as the emperor's doctor examined his wound. "And I will ask God to forgive you. All I ask in return is that you spare my friends, the animals that live in this forest."

"I will not harm that doe, nor any other animal that dwells in this forest," the emperor vowed. "I will never hunt here again."

Charlemagne kept his promise. Giles recovered from his wound and went on to establish many churches and monasteries.

Saint Giles's feast day is September 1. His emblem is the white doe, after the deer he rescued from the hunters. Because he suffered from his arrow wound, he is the patron saint of all who experience physical suffering, especially the physically handicapped.

Saint Hormisdas
and the Camels

PERSIA—FIFTH CENTURY

Saint Hormisdas came from a noble family, one of the wealthiest in Persia. Unlike their neighbors, Hormisdas and his parents were Christians.

The king of Persia went to war with the neighboring Christian kingdom of Byzantium. The king feared that the Persian Christians might be supporting his enemies secretly. He decided to do away with them.

All Christians living in the land of Persia were given a choice. They could either abandon their religion or be put to death.

Hormisdas and his family were among those arrested. He saw his parents led away to execution. The king offered to spare the boy, on the condition that he renounce his religion. Hormisdas refused. The king decided to break his spirit by sending him to work as a stable boy for the royal camels.

It was a cruel punishment for a nobleman's son who had never known hard labor. Hormisdas lugged buckets of water, shoveled mountains of manure, hauled heaps of fodder. Keeping the stalls clean was an endless task. Even the camels seemed to persecute him. They kicked and bit him whenever they could.

Worst of all was an old camel named Ahriman. He never missed an opportunity to attack Hormisdas. The boy's body was black-and-blue with bruises from Ahriman's kicks. Scars from the camel's bites covered Hormisdas's arms. The wicked beast even fouled his stall just before it was to be inspected, as if he knew that Hormisdas would be punished for not doing his work properly.

Yet the boy never complained. He spoke gently to the camels, and

sang to them, praising God with every word, even though Ahriman drowned out his words with thunderous snorts and bellows.

One day the grooms found Ahriman lying in his stall. The old camel was dying. "This nasty brute is finished at last," the grooms said. "Good riddance! Let's finish him off and haul his ugly carcass away."

Only Hormisdas felt sad to see the dying camel. He carried a bucket of water into the stall. Kneeling by Ahriman's head, he pressed a wet cloth to the camel's lips. Ahriman drank slowly, drop by drop, as Hormisdas begged God to help the camel.

Suddenly Ahriman snorted. He raised his head, rolled to his knees, and got up. He charged at the grooms, who fell over one another trying to get out of the stall. Only Hormisdas did not run away. He held out his hand to the camel.

"Get out, Hormisdas! Ahriman will kill you!" the grooms shouted.

But the camel didn't bite or kick. He lowered his head to let Hormisdas scratch his ears.

From then on Hormisdas and Ahriman became close friends. Ahriman would not allow the other camels to abuse Hormisdas. The grooms began to treat the boy kindly too for fear of angering Ahriman.

When the king heard about the miracle, he gave Hormisdas one last chance to renounce his religion. When the boy again refused, the king ordered him put to death, along with the camel. Hormisdas and Ahriman died together.

Saint Hormisdas is the patron saint of grooms and stable boys. His emblem is the camel, and his feast day is August 8.

Saint Hubert and the Stag

FRANCE—SEVENTH TO EIGHTH CENTURY

Hubert was a high-spirited noble youth in the court of the king of France. He had an ear for gossip and an eye for fine clothes and fair ladies. When not feasting or dancing, he devoted himself to hunting, his greatest pleasure.

One morning, while riding out with his friends from court, he encountered a hermit standing in the middle of the path. "Hubert! Where are you going?" the hermit cried.

"I'm going hunting, you foolish fellow!" the young nobleman said, and laughed.

"It is a sin to spend this holy day chasing after worldly pleasures. Do you not know that today is Good Friday, the day our Lord died on the cross to save all humankind from suffering and death?"

"I'm grateful for that," Hubert said. "But I still don't see why I should spend the day mumbling prayers and crawling about on my knees. Since the good Lord has sent us such fine hunting weather, I say it would be a sin to waste it." Hubert spurred his horse and rode on, leaving the poor hermit behind in a cloud of dust.

Hubert's hounds soon picked up the scent of a stag. Hubert blew his hunting horn to summon his companions. They followed the trail deeper and deeper into the forest. From time to time, they caught sight of the stag. He was as tall and as powerfully muscled as a warhorse. A rack of antlers like a forest of spears crowned his head. Hubert had never seen such a magnificent animal. He vowed that he would be the one to bring him down.

Hubert galloped ahead of his companions. He followed the stag through a tangle of ancient oaks.

Hubert stopped at the edge of a clearing. The stag stood facing him. Hubert fitted an arrow into his bowstring and took careful aim.

What strange magic was this? The image of Christ on the cross appeared, floating in the air between the stag's antlers. The shining figure on the cross spoke to him.

"Woe to you, Hubert! You have wasted your life on vanity and idle pleasure. What will become of you?"

The bow dropped from Hubert's hands. He heard the baying of his hounds and turned in the saddle to look for them. When he gazed back again, the stag and the holy image between his antlers had vanished.

Hubert and his companions caught nothing that day. They rode home in silence. The other young nobles asked Hubert why he suddenly had become so solemn, why he no longer laughed and joked. Hubert did not answer. His thoughts weighed heavy on his heart. He told no one what he had seen. He never went hunting again.

Hubert vowed to make himself worthy of his vision. It was the only way to give his life meaning. Hubert became a priest. He helped the poor and sick. He built hospitals and churches.

Hubert, the hunter who became a saint, is remembered as one of France's great leaders. His feast day is November 3. His emblem is the stag. He is the patron saint of hunters.

Saint Hugh
and the Swan

ENGLAND—TWELFTH CENTURY

Bishop Hugh of Lincoln loved animals. He had a pet swan that followed him everywhere. Hugh liked to hide tidbits in the wide sleeves of his bishop's robe. He would laugh when the swan ran its long neck up his sleeves, clacking its beak, looking for the treats. The swan walked beside Bishop Hugh when he led processions around the Lincoln cathedral on holy days. The bird waddled along solemnly, bowing its neck to the left and right, as if it were one of the high churchmen of England.

Lincoln had a large Jewish community. Jews in England were a persecuted minority. They were forced to wear yellow badges, live in special districts, and pay heavy taxes.

Bishop Hugh felt pity for the Jews. He could not change the unfair laws under which they lived, but he could protect them from the worst of their oppressors.

One day rumors began circulating throughout Lincoln that the Jews had insulted the Christian religion. Angry crowds began gathering in the streets, demanding that all the Jews in the city be put to death.

Hugh had heard these rumors before. He knew they were lies. He told the Jews of Lincoln to come to the cathedral. He vowed to protect them or die in the attempt.

The angry mob gathered at the entrance to the cathedral. Hugh met them at the door. "Go home!" he said. "Lincoln's Jews are under my protection. They are guilty of no crime. Don't believe wicked rumors. Do not shed innocent blood."

The mob's leaders told Hugh to get out of the way. They threatened to drag the Jews out and burn them alive in the town square.

"You will have to burn me too," said the bishop, standing fast.

At that moment the swan came waddling out of the cathedral, looking for its friend. The bird did not understand what this fuss was about; it only knew that it was hungry and it was time for treats. The swan thrust its long neck up Hugh's sleeve while the bishop tried to reason with the mob. People began to laugh. So did Bishop Hugh. Soon the whole crowd was chortling.

"Look here, good people," Hugh said. "We should all have the sense of this bird. The hour is late. It is time for dinner. The swan is hungry. I am hungry. You must be hungry too. Let us all go home and forget this foolishness."

The people of Lincoln finally came to see reason. The crowd dispersed, the people went home, and Lincoln's Jews were saved. Bishop Hugh and his swan went back inside the cathedral. The swan got extra treats that day, because whether the bird knew it or not, it had done a very great deed.

Saint Hugh, who had compassion for all who suffered, is the patron saint of sick children. His emblem is the swan, and his feast day is November 17.

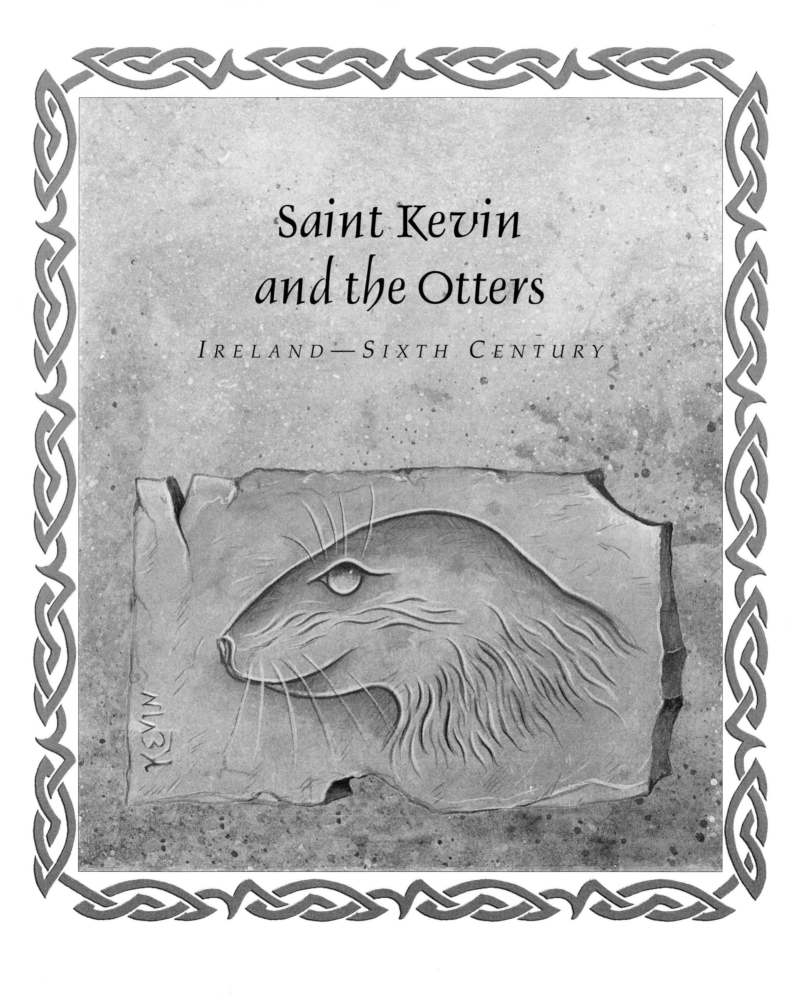

Saint Kevin
and the Otters

IRELAND—SIXTH CENTURY

Saint Kevin lived as a hermit in a cave overlooking the lake of Glendalough. Birds and wild animals were his only companions. Kevin had loved animals since he was a small boy. He always treated them with kindness and compassion.

Kevin devoted himself to holiness. He fasted for days at a time, filling his hours with prayer and meditation. Tales of the holy hermit of Glendalough spread through the countryside. Young men from all over Ireland came to the lake to be close to Kevin so that they might draw strength from his holiness and wisdom.

Kevin, who wanted to be a solitary hermit, found himself the leader of a community of monks. How was he to feed all these people? The country folk of the district were poor farmers and fishermen. They had nothing to give. Kevin knelt beside the lake. He prayed to God for an answer.

Lifting his eyes, he saw a family of otters swimming toward him. Each otter held a struggling salmon. The otters pulled the salmon onshore. They laid the fish before Kevin. Then they jumped back into the lake to catch more.

Kevin fed his followers with the salmon the otters caught for him. None of the monks ever went hungry, unless they happened to be observing a fast. The otters seemed to know when the monks were fasting. They brought no salmon on those days.

Saint Kevin, along with Saint Patrick, is one of Ireland's patron saints. His feast day is June 3. His emblem is the otter.

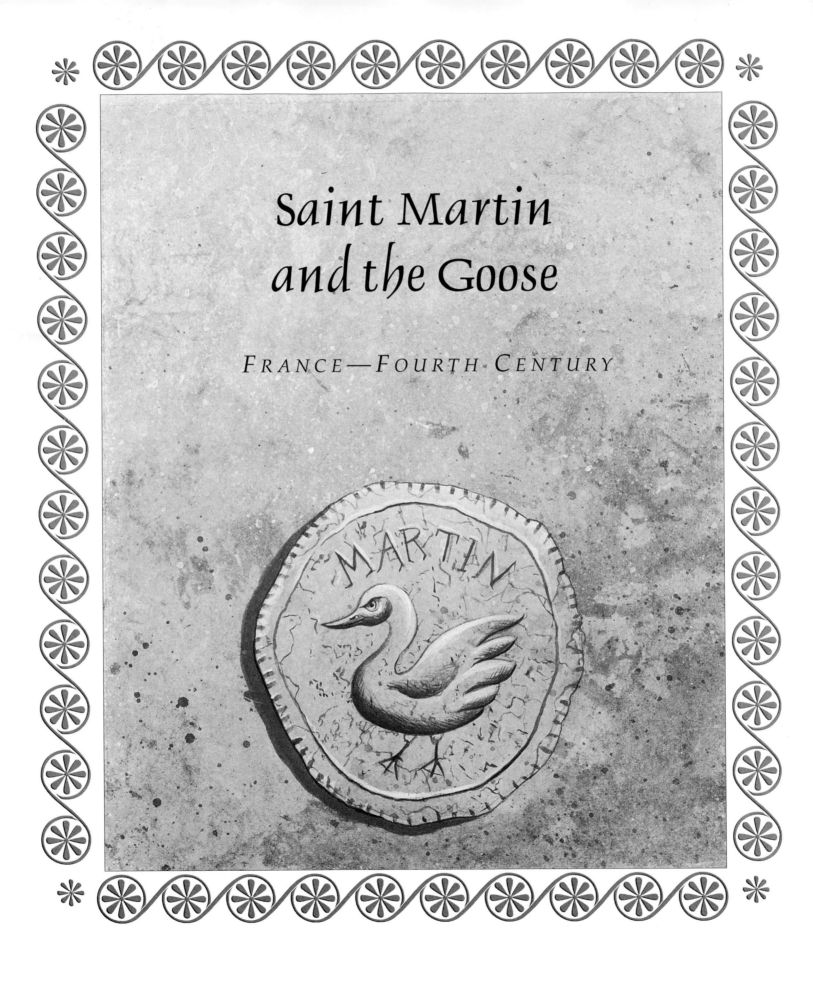

Saint Martin
and the Goose

France—Fourth Century

Saint Martin of Tours grew up on the outskirts of the Roman Empire, in the province of Pannonia, which is now called Hungary. Martin grew up to become a famous horseman, renowned for his ability to tame the wildest stallions. He did it without using spurs, whips, or cruel bridles. Martin's gentle voice and sure, easy touch convinced the most uncontrollable horses that here was a human being they could trust.

Martin was drafted into the Roman cavalry when he was still a teenager. While serving in France, he realized that he wanted to become a Christian. Yet somehow he hesitated to take the final step.

One freezing winter day, while on patrol near the city of Amiens, Martin came upon a beggar standing in the snow. The poor man was dressed in rags. He had no coat, not even a blanket, to protect him from the bitter cold. Moved to pity by the beggar's suffering, Martin took off his cloak—which was big enough to cover himself and his horse—and cut it in half with his sword. He gave one half to the beggar and continued on his way.

That night Martin had a dream. He saw Jesus himself, naked and bleeding, wrapped in the part of his cloak that he had given to the beggar. As soon as the sun rose, Martin hurried to the nearest church and asked to be received into the Christian faith.

Martin left the army and became a priest. His kindness, holiness, and ability to work miracles inspired many others to convert to Christianity. The people of the town of Tours wanted Martin to become their bishop.

That was the last thing Martin wanted. Being a bishop would be like being back in the army. He would have to go to meetings, settle arguments, and raise money. He would be busy from morning to night, with never a minute for quiet prayer.

Martin wanted no part of such a life, so he hid in the forest. The people of Tours searched for him everywhere. No one could find him. What had become of Martin? everyone wondered.

One of those who asked that question was a goose boy named Bertrand. Every morning he led his flock to the lake and brought it home in the evening. One evening he noticed that one of his geese was missing. It was his favorite, a slender bird called Blanche. Bertrand felt sick at heart, worrying that she might have fallen prey to a fox. He hurried home with the rest of the flock and returned to the lake to search for her.

Bertrand walked around the shore of the lake, calling for Blanche. The sun was going down. Soon he would have to give up the search. "Blanche! Blanche!" he called one last time.

Bertrand heard a faint honking. It came from an island in the middle of the lake. The water was not deep. Bertrand waded across. There he found Blanche, waddling around an oak tree, looking up into its branches.

"Honk! Honk!" The goose flapped her wings. *"Honk! Honk!"* she called again.

"Go away, you silly bird! Leave me in peace!" hissed a voice.

"That's no goose!" said Bertrand. He looked up into the tree. "Who's there?" To his surprise, he saw Martin sitting on one of the branches.

"Bishop Martin! What are you doing here? Everyone is looking for you!"

"Don't call me bishop. I'm not your bishop. I don't want to be a bishop. Take your goose and go away!"

"Bishop Martin, haven't you taught us to do God's will, even if it is not what we would prefer for ourselves?" asked Bertrand.

"What are you trying to tell me?"

"What I meant to say," Bertrand began, "is that if God wanted you to be a hermit in the forest, He wouldn't have sent Blanche to find you. He wouldn't have sent me to find Blanche. And He wouldn't have sent you to be our bishop."

"You are right," Martin finally agreed. "God appeared to Saint Paul on the way to Damascus. Saint Peter encountered Our Lord on the road from Rome. I am not as worthy as they; God only sends me a goose. However, the message is more important than the messenger. Thank you, Bertrand, and thank you, Blanche, for showing me the way. Go tell the people of Tours that I will be their bishop."

Blanche stretched out her neck and flapped her wings. *"Honk! Honk!"* she proclaimed joyously.

Because of his early life as a cavalryman, Saint Martin is the patron saint of beggars, soldiers, horses, and all who enjoy equestrian sports. One of his emblems is the goose, recalling the goose that found his hiding place in the forest. That is why roast goose is traditionally served at Martinmas, Saint Martin's feast day. Because Martinmas falls on November 11, any spell of unseasonably fine weather in late October or early November is called Saint Martin's summer.

Saint Notburga and the Pigs

AUSTRIA—THIRTEENTH TO FOURTEENTH CENTURY

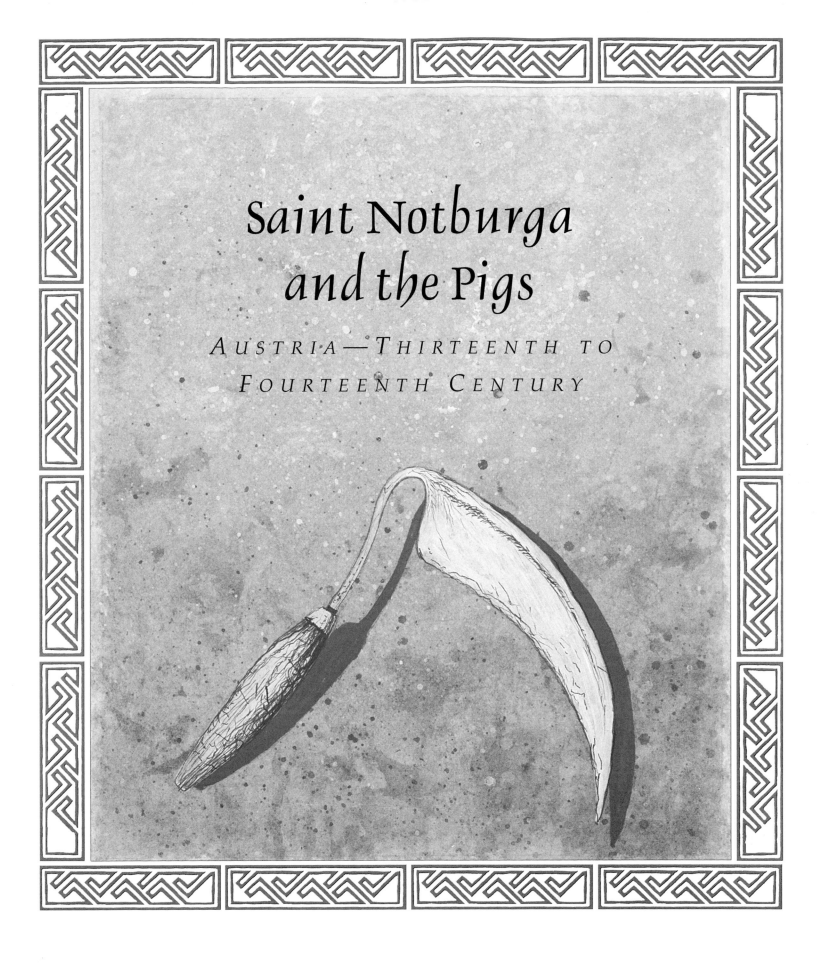

Saint Notburga's parents were poor farmers who had more children than they could feed. When Notburga was a little girl, her mother and father brought her to Rattenberg castle to work for the count and countess in exchange for food and clothing.

Notburga's day began before dawn and ended long after sundown. She did work that no one else wanted to do. She scrubbed stone floors. She scraped out drains and privies. She climbed up chimneys to brush out soot. She hauled heaps of garbage.

Despite her endless drudgery, Notburga never complained. She sang to herself as she went about her chores. She said her prayers every night before she went to sleep, asking God to bless Count Henry and Countess Ottilia for their kindness to her.

Count Henry held a great feast every night for his friends. There was always more to eat than there were people to eat it.

One of Notburga's nightly chores was to carry out the wasted food and dump it in a pit. She thought to herself, It is a pity to waste such good food when so many people have nothing to eat. She began telling the needy people who came to the castle to meet her after dark by the gate. She let them take as much as they wanted from the food she was throwing away.

Notburga fed all the poor people of Rattenberg with food that the count and countess discarded. One day the bishop came to the castle to thank Count Henry for his kindness. His visit surprised the count, for he knew nothing about Notburga's good deed. The countess, however, became irate.

"How dare that kitchen scullion give away our food!" she screamed at her husband after the bishop left.

"What harm is there?" Count Henry answered. "The extra food would have been tossed in the garbage pit anyway. Let the poor enjoy it."

"The poor can fend for themselves," snapped Countess Ottilia. "Give the leftovers to our pigs. They will get fat, and then we can eat them. Nothing will be wasted."

Count Henry feared his wife's sharp tongue, so he made no attempt to argue. The countess ordered that all leftover food be brought to the pigs. Not one crumb was to be given away to the poor.

Notburga had to obey. Each evening she carried wasted food to the pigpen. The pigs would not touch it. They seemed to say, "Pigs we may be, but we are still not as greedy as the countess of Rattenberg."

Notburga could not let uneaten food rot. She took it out through the gate to the trash pit. She let the poor take what they pleased. Soon Notburga was feeding as many of the poor people as before.

When the countess learned of this, she ordered her husband to send Notburga away. The count did so with regret, for he admired Notburga's generosity and kindness.

Notburga went to work for a farmer in a nearby village. She told him, "I will work hard and do whatever you ask. I only require one thing in return. Do not make me work on Sunday. Sunday belongs to God."

Notburga was working in the field one Saturday afternoon when she heard church bells ringing. It was time for vespers. She put down her sickle and started walking to church.

"Where are you going?" the farmer called to her.

"I don't work on the Sabbath," Notburga said.

"Sunday is tomorrow," the farmer replied.

"The Sabbath begins in the evening with vespers. The vesper bells are calling us to church."

"Pick up that sickle and get back to work!" said the farmer.

"Let God decide if I am right or wrong." Notburga tossed the sickle high into the air, where it hung like a crescent moon. She continued on to church, leaving the astonished farmer staring at the sky.

When the Sabbath ended, Notburga received an urgent message from Count Henry. Countess Ottilia had died. Her ghost haunted the pigsty, calling Notburga's name.

Notburga entered the pigsty. She saw Countess Ottilia's ghost standing in the muck and mire, with pigs rooting at her feet.

"Help me, Notburga!" the spirit groaned.

"Why are you here?" Notburga asked.

"Because I gave the poor people's food to my pigs, I have been condemned to spend eternity in this pigsty. It was wicked of me to deny starving people food that was going to be thrown away. Now I must pay for my sins."

"I will pray for you," said Notburga. She fell to her knees and asked God to forgive the countess. "Let whatever blessings I earned by feeding the poor be given to her. Remember, it was her food, not mine, that fed them."

Notburga finished her prayer. The ghost disappeared, never to return.

Saint Notburga is the patron saint of poor farmers and hired servants. Her feast day is September 14. Her emblem is the sickle.

Author's Note

What are saints? Saints are people whose lives exhibit such special holiness that others continue to ask for their help even after they are dead.

Canonization is the process by which a person becomes recognized as a saint. It begins after a candidate's death. The person's life and deeds are carefully evaluated. If the church authorities approve, the pope declares the candidate "venerable," meaning "worthy of reverence."

The next step, beatification, requires convincing evidence that the candidate has performed at least one miracle. When this is confirmed, the pope proclaims the candidate "beatified," or "blessed."

If evidence can be found that the candidate has performed a second miracle, the pope may proceed to the third step, canonization. Canonization means that the church officially recognizes the person as a saint.

This process does not make a person a saint. Only God can do that. Through canonization, the church recognizes what God has already done.